THE BUSINESS
BEASTIARY

THE BUSINESS
BEASTIARY

Arthur Hecht
Byron Stevens

Illustrated by Jack Medoff

A SCARBOROUGH BOOK
STEIN AND DAY/*Publishers*/New York

First published in 1982
Copyright © 1982 by Arthur Hecht
All rights reserved
Designed by Louis A. Ditizio
Printed in the United States of America
STEIN AND DAY/*Publishers*
Scarborough House
Briarcliff Manor, N.Y. 10510

CONTENTS

THE BUSINESS
BEASTIARY

A Prefatory Word

Once upon a time, back in the Middle Ages, monks with a little spare time on their hands amused themselves by inventing *bestiaries*. Bestiaries were books that contained fanciful descriptions of animals everybody believed in at the time, like unicorns, gryphons, and chimeras. They also contained imaginative versions of animals nobody believed in back then, such as camels, giraffes, and hippopotami.

Believing in hippos is still a matter of individual preference, but the point is that the world has changed a lot since the days when anybody listened to what a monk said about a giraffe.

Today's beasts are of a very different order. Anyone who's ever spent time in today's business jungle knows that it's beastly, not bestly. So we're calling this book a beastiary, not a bestiary. That's beast as in "You Beast!" and "Beast of Prey." Wishing all the best ...

—The Authors

9

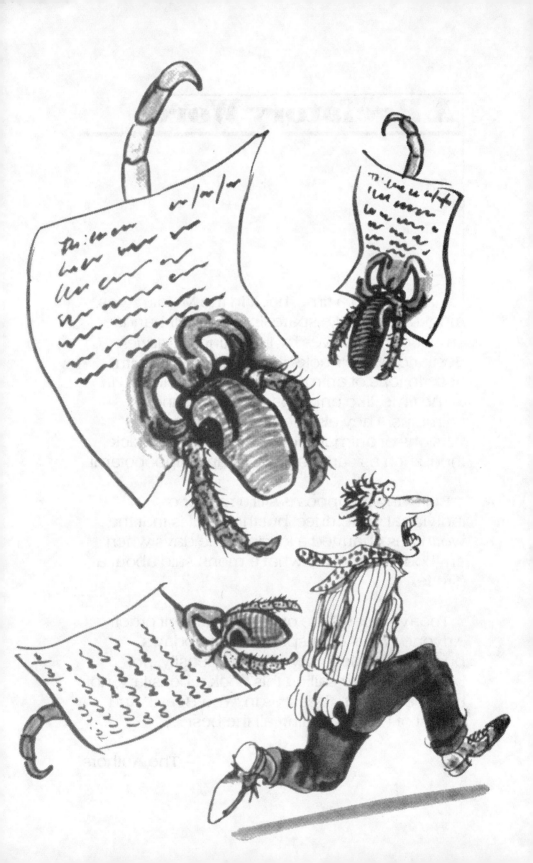

The Interoffice Memo

The Interoffice Memo is an insectlike creature that flits from desk to desk carrying a sting. Like June Bugs and Fireflies, it has an active life of only one or two days. It then goes into a dormant stage in a suspense file, before re-emerging during the season of squabbles and disputes.

Like all insects, Interoffice Memos proliferate very quickly. No sooner do you turn one of them loose than the whole office fills up with them. Most insects, however, have one face, whereas this creature almost always has two. Interoffice Memos are also unusual in that they cannot reproduce without the aid of a machine. They have a talent for stating the obvious in an awkward way, and they show a fierce, primordial instinct to cover their hindquarters at all costs.

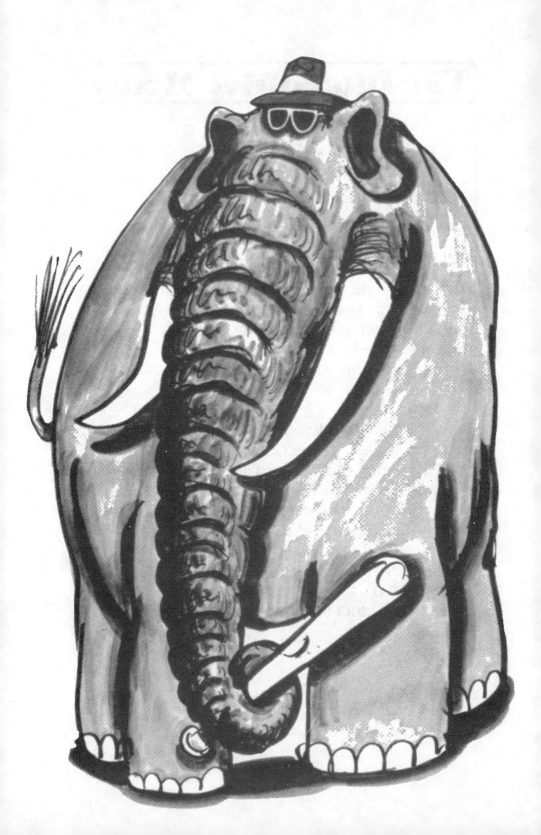

The Account Payable

An Account Payable is another name for an animal better known as the Unpaid Bill. This is a beast that even ordinary people have a lot of experience with. If the kid who delivers your newspapers has started telling you that his uncle is a lawyer and his big brother rides a motorcycle, you've just learned something essential about what happens to an Account Payable as it gets older.

As you might guess, Accounts Payable are very common animals. You'll know one when you see it, because an Account Payable is usually inconveniently large and is nearly always encountered at an awkward moment. There is an old saying in the business world that one man's Account Payable is another man's Receivable. What this means is that regardless of who gets the short end of the stick, the stick itself is always the same size.

13

The Mailed Check

One of the oddities of doing business in this country is that the Postal Service seems to be so much more careless handling Checks than handling Bills. This situation has created one of the common varmints of the business world, the Mailed Check. Like beauty, this beast exists only in the eye of the beholder. Mailed Checks are notorious animals, but are not likely to be exterminated because they please precisely as many people as they upset.

Mailed Checks are feeble and flimsy and virtually transparent, which is why most businessmen see through them right away. They are frequently seen leaving an establishment, but far less frequently seen arriving. When they do arrive, they are often postdated, sometimes lacking a signature, and it is almost always after three o'clock on a Friday afternoon.

The MBA

In recent years, the proliferation of MBAs in this country has been staggering. No one knows quite what to do with all of them, but everybody agrees that these creatures represent an amazing evolutionary development. The MBA has not evolved the ability to perform or hold any job in particular; instead it is marvelously adapted to simply *finding* a job in the first place.

MBAs are very systematic animals. They believe in grids, graphs, charts, timetables, formulas, and marketing plans. In fact, one of the first things you'll notice about an MBA is that it has a system for doing all the things it has never done before. MBAs appear to have their own language (in which "interface" is a word and "access" is a verb), and they claim to have their own ideas. They are like trainees but cost a lot more money.

The Income Tax

This is an animal that eats discretionary income. It is the natural enemy of the Profit, which is why Profits are so often seen trying to disguise themselves as Costs and Expenses.

According to folklore, there once was a time when the Income Tax did not exist. The story goes that back around the turn of the century, Congress bred this creature to give CPAs a reason for living. Since then, the Income Tax has evolved into a gigantic and very powerful animal that has a small and very bureaucratic brain. Income Taxes can be fed on three plans: the annual plan, the estimated plan, and the jail plan.

The Audit

Audits are without doubt the most dreaded beasts in the business jungle. They are said to attack at random and to kill for pleasure. Relentless hunters with insatiable appetites, they have fangs and a keen sense of smell, and they like to gorge themselves on undocumented expenditures. In fact, the only thing worse than an Audit is the fear of an Audit.

If you suspect an Audit might be in the area, lie low and hope it's your neighbor that gets bitten.

Credit

Credit isn't precisely an animal . . . it's a social disease. Scientists are divided on the question of whether Credit is viral or bacterial, but everybody agrees that it's not infectious. If you already have it, you can probably get more of it, but if you don't have it to begin with, you won't catch it no matter how hard you try.

The Profit

Profits are prestigious and highly sought-after animals. There are a great many varieties of Profits, including the Gross, the Net, the Negligible, the Windfall, and the Obscene. The Gross Profit is what you look at before you decide on showing a net loss; the Net Profit is whatever you think the I.R.S. will believe; the Negligible Profit is what you let on to your customers; the Windfall Profit is a figment of the public imagination; and the Obscene Profit is generally somebody else's.

Not too long ago, Profits of all sorts were plentiful in this country. Today they are increasingly scarce and are found mostly in a few preserves, such as IBM and Exxon. One theory has it that the economic climate does not always agree with the Profit, but another possibility is that, as with the Bison, too many people made killings.

The Budget

When God created two people and only one apple, He created the Budget. Budgets are grouchy, uncooperative animals that are colored variously in red and black. They come in all sizes, but no matter how big a Budget is, it never seems big enough.

Like secondhand cars, Budgets are prone to problems. A Budget that has learned how to juggle is known as a Balanced Budget. As Budgets get older, however, they are more likely to turn into Deficits. The exception is the Federal Budget, which *begins* life as a Deficit and is a Budget in name only.

The Estimate

Estimates are moderately sized animals that grow at a tremendous rate whenever they are not being watched. These beasts have good imaginations. They also have very poor memories.

The kind of Estimate most often sought is the Exact, but the one most often found is the Rough. Rough Estimates start off smaller than Exact ones, but they grow to be much larger in time.

There is another variety of this animal called the Absurd Estimate. These can be either Absurdly Low or Absurdly High. Absurdly Low Estimates are frequently found in municipal contracts. Absurdly High Estimates are found in auto repair shops, where they are bred for the purpose of entertaining insurance companies.

The Forecast

Forecasts are predictable animals. They always want to know what's coming down, whether it's interest rates or six inches of snow. As with eggs and fairies, there are Good Forecasts and Bad Forecasts. Unfortunately, in the business world they are increasingly difficult to distinguish.

These are seasonal beasts, and while they are abundant at the beginning of each fiscal year, they are rarely seen at the end of it. As anyone familiar with the Bible will tell you, Forecasts are born of Dreams. Young Forecasts are called Timetables, but as they mature, people start calling them Guesstimates instead. An old Forecast is usually referred to as a Learning Experience.

The Inflation

Like Howard Cosell, Inflation is a creature that nobody wants but that seems to be everywhere anyway. There are two species of Inflation, the Checked and the Unchecked. The Checked Inflation is very rare these days, and experts fear it may be dying out, possibly because it suffers from fits of depression.

The Unchecked Inflation, however, is alive and kicking and moving along as fast as a Cheetah chasing Jesse Owens. Unchecked Inflations have been described as Unbridled, Galloping, Runaway, Ascending, Spiraling, Skyrocketing, and even Awe-Inspiring.

Nonetheless, Politicians are always promising to bring the beast under control. It is well known that the only way to control this animal is not to feed it, but unfortunately when you starve an Inflation everything around it starves, too.

The Operating Expense

Operating Expenses come in all shapes and sizes, but no matter what size they are, they are always larger than anticipated. Telephone bills, secretarial salaries, and payola are all Operating Expenses.

Operating Expenses are classified as being either High or Low. Thus, a company that wants to strip-mine on top of Mt. Rushmore is going to have a particularly High Operating Expense, whereas a teenager sharing pot with his friends at somewhat above his cost will have a comparatively Low Operating Expense.

The Committee

Committees are creatures that have too many heads and not enough thoughts. This is why it takes them so long to decide on doing whatever the Chairman wanted to do in the first place. These animals may be found wherever there is a problem that no one person wants to risk being blamed for. They feed on a garbled mixture of input, and they respond by producing output, sometimes in the form of resolutions and always in motions to adjourn.

Committees are much maligned animals, and it is widely rumored that they can't even answer a telephone. It has been said that a Camel is a Horse designed by a Committee. What is not said as often is that a Committee is a Solution designed by a Horse.

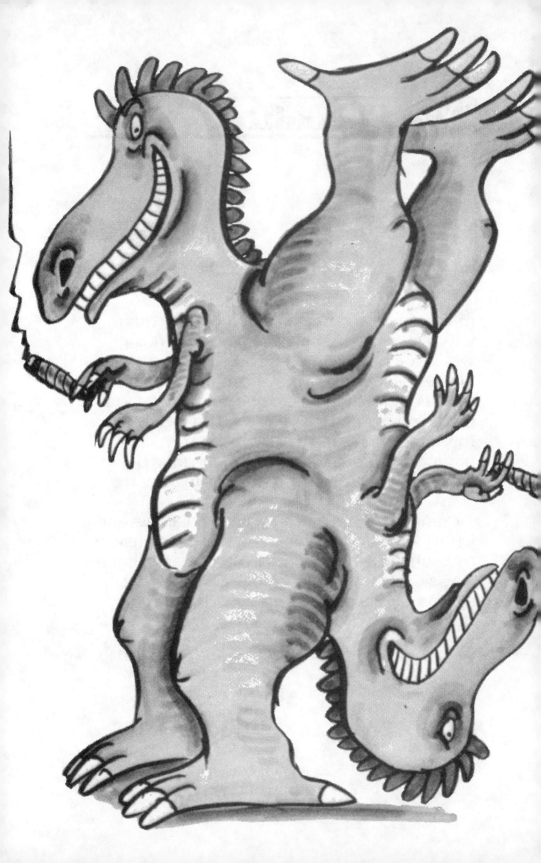

The Entrepreneur

Entrepreneurs are among the most energetic animals in the business community. They tend to be young, though not quite as young as they used to be, and people generally think highly of them, though not quite as highly as they think of themselves. They are daring and ambitious, and they have a lot of ideas about how to spend somebody else's money. In fact, an Entrepreneur can smell out the Venture Capital like a Shark smelling blood in the sea.

Like any beast, these animals have an up side and a down side. On the up side, Entrepreneurs are the heart and soul of the economy, the C.E.O.s of tomorrow's corporations. On the down side, they are poor credit risks and are usually getting a divorce from some other animal. They can't take "no" for an answer, and they hate having to say "yes" to anybody. Essentially, an Entrepreneur is an animal that was so hard to get along with it had to go into business for itself.

The C.E.O.

The Chief Executive Officer is a creature that shows an amazing ability to survive times of stress by feeding exclusively on cottage cheese and scotch. C.E.O.s are migratory animals. Good places for sighting them are New York and Los Angeles (weekdays, Fridays until noon), as well as Aspen and Easthampton (weekends, Sundays not before noon).

C.E.O.s, like Tigers and Barracudas, are firm believers in the primacy of their turf. They establish their territories not by urinating around its perimeter but by refusing to take one another's phone calls and by breaking one another's appointments.

The Certified Public Accountant

The C.P.A. is a pale, hairless, backward-looking little animal that has absolutely no sense of humor. The C.P.A. sometimes goes through a larval stage as a Bookkeeper. C.P.A.s are born wearing glasses and the wrong-colored shirt. They breed at the end of each fiscal year, but much of what they do is sterile.

C.P.A.s are unique in their ability to become emotionally involved with computers, and they are the only animals that have ever been automated without being replaced.

The Attorney

There are very few things in life that can be shared between a Businessman and a Child Molester: A Lawyer is one of them. Sooner or later, every businessman will think he needs one of these Law Creatures, but it behooves him to remember that they are fed at 15-minute intervals.

The Attorney thrives on the misfortunes of others. If there are not enough misfortunes around, Attorneys are capable of creating them for each other. They may have sharp beaks and are often bald. They have talons and a powerful grip, and they cannot be satisfied with less than an arm and a leg. Though Attorneys tend to see themselves as Eagles, people often think of them as Vultures. While some people think that the Insect may eventually take over the world, in many places Attorneys are coming in a close second.

The Consultant

Consultants are animals that charge others for the benefit of their companionship. They are known for their tractable dispositions, and they devote a lot of attention to ritual grooming. Consultants might not be in the world's oldest profession, but if not they certainly caught on fast.

Most of these animals have just left the business jungle in order to tell others how to stay in it. Like Actors, they are often between jobs, and like Psychiatrists, they are a paid audience. A Consultant is what you hire when you want to spend money making up your own mind.

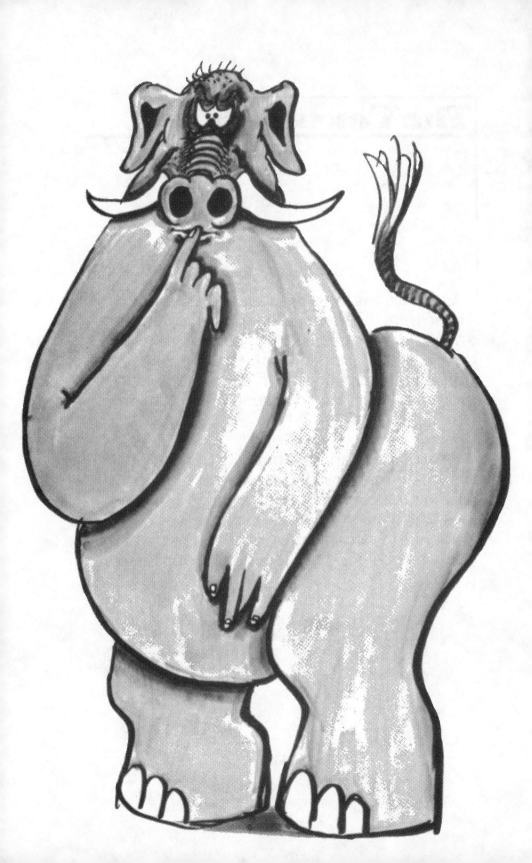

The Silent Partner

As their name implies, Silent Partners are creatures normally found in the company of others, known as Active Partners (also known as Babbling Partners, Front-Men, or Shills). Like Swans, Silent Partners speak but once. This is known as testimony and occurs just before the partnership dies.

Teddy Roosevelt believed in speaking softly and carrying a big stick—Silent Partners believe in saying nothing at all and retaining a big law firm. Silent Partners should not be confused with Silenced Partners, which are different animals altogether, and which are found with some regularity in deserted portions of the Jersey swamps.

The Headhunter

It is well known in the business world that if you want to get ahead, you're going to need a head to begin with, unless you can arrange to use somebody else's. Naturally, this has created a real demand for Headhunters, and immigration quotas from New Guinea being what they are, it is a Hunter's market here at home.

This creature has tentacles, which it prefers to call connections, and one enormous ear, which it keeps to the ground. Headhunters understand instinctively that they must collect and turn over as many heads as possible. Of course, if you place all those heads, you have a lot of tails left over, but that flesh gets peddled in another part of town.

The Bottom Line

One of the constant questions in business is: "What does the Bottom Line look like?" Considering that businessmen come face to face with this creature every day, this might seem like an odd thing to ask, but the fact is that Bottom Lines are always changing their appearance. Thus, this is a large or small, fat or scrawny, happy or sad animal, and the next time you hear a businessman talking about the long and the short of it, you can bet your bottom dollar he's referring to the Bottom Line.

The Annual Report

Annual Reports usually have a good sense of theater and no sense of shame. Like Poodles and Circus Ponies, they are performing animals. Once each fiscal year, the Annual Report trots out into the spotlight and amazes stockholders with its ability to comprehend statistics and its inability to comprehend reality.

These animals pride themselves on their extraordinary vision. They have insight, second-sight, and hindsight. Though Annual Reports claim to see into tomorrow, oddly enough they have trouble reading the writing on the wall.

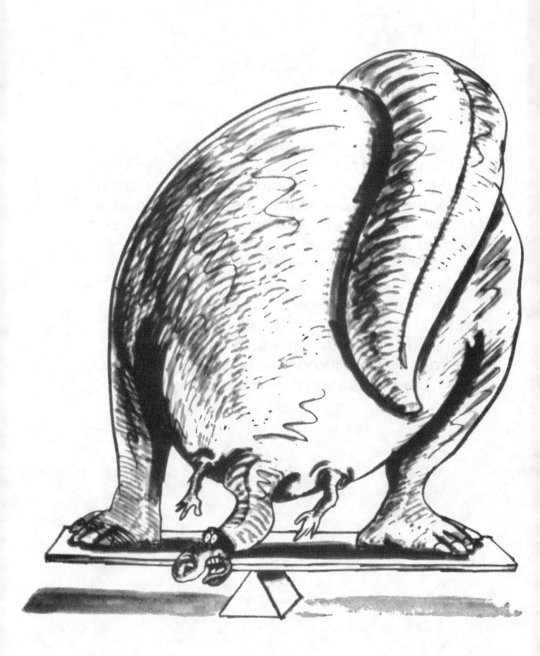

The Balance Sheet

The Balance Sheet is a beast that can be paper trained at a very early age. This is just one reason why Bankers love this animal better than Dogs. Of course, some Balance Sheets look so much like Dogs that it's tough to tell the difference.

These creatures have the best sense of equilibrium in the animal kingdom. A Balance Sheet in good form can simultaneously walk an economic tightrope and juggle several sets of books. What counts though are the ratios. The Balance Sheet is the only animal that looks best when its left upper side looks swollen compared to its right upper side.

The Frozen Asset

The Frozen Asset is a victim of life's circumstances. Through no default of its own, this loveable, lighthearted, and liquid creature was tied down by legal entanglements and frozen on the spot. Of course, the thing most likely to change a Liquid Asset into a frozen one is a harsh economic climate. In fact, if matters get much worse, a lot of people are going to wind up with their Assets frozen off.

The Barter

Barters are crafty little animals that like their markets black and their customers green. These beasts are famous for their ability to practice magic. They can make a Profit invisible, and they can saw a Sales Tax in half. They can also transform a sport shirt into a sport car without needlessly inconveniencing the government.

Barters are among the most ancient of all business beasts. They evolved at the dawn of civilization, when conditions on this earth were far from hospitable. Because of this, Barters are able to flourish during famines, plagues, and world wars. They also do very well during periods of confiscatory taxation, which is why they are so popular today.

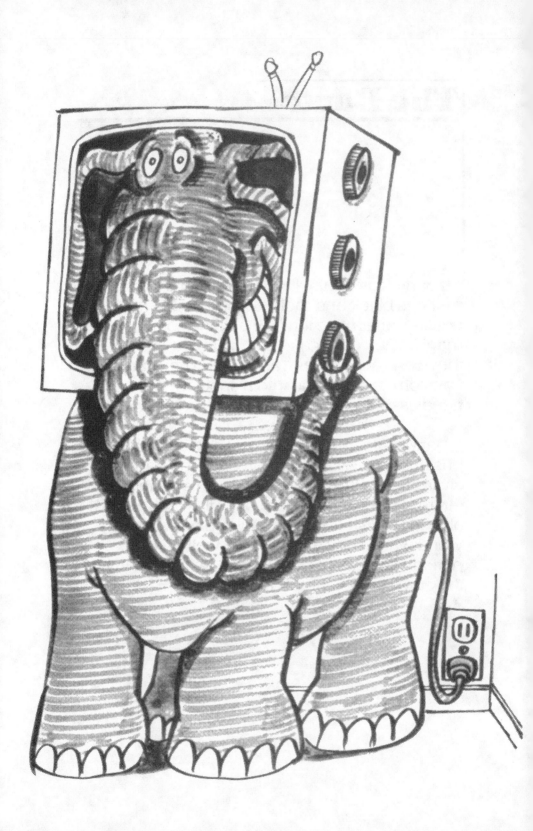

The Advertisement

Advertisements are like elephants—you not only have to spend more than you might think for the beast itself, you have to pay big money just for the space to put it in.

The Venture Capital

Venture Capitals are gorgeous animals with glossy coats and pedicured claws. However, they are also very nervous animals, since so many of them die horrible deaths at a young age. These creatures must live by their wits, and they are typically daring, brash, determined, self-confident, cocky, aggressive, and intoxicated.

These animals have great faith in their ability to calculate risk, and they are fond of the expression, "It takes money to make money." Of course, as every investor knows, it takes money to lose money, too. An odd thing about the Venture Capital is that nearly everybody prefers to use somebody else's.

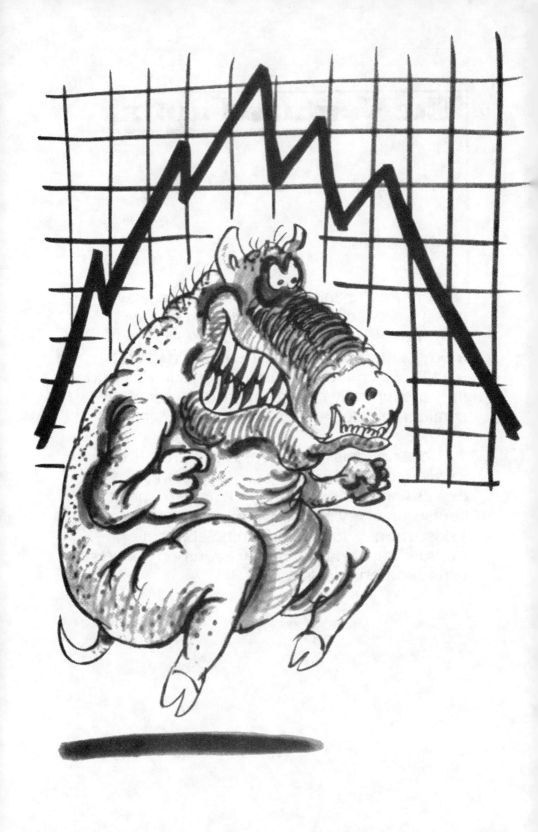

The Securities

Securities, sometimes known as Insecurities, include Stocks, Bonds, and Commodity Futures. These animals are all the offspring of Sir Isaac Newton, the man who discovered gravity. As Sir Isaac observed, what goes up must come down, but what comes down might never get off the ground again.

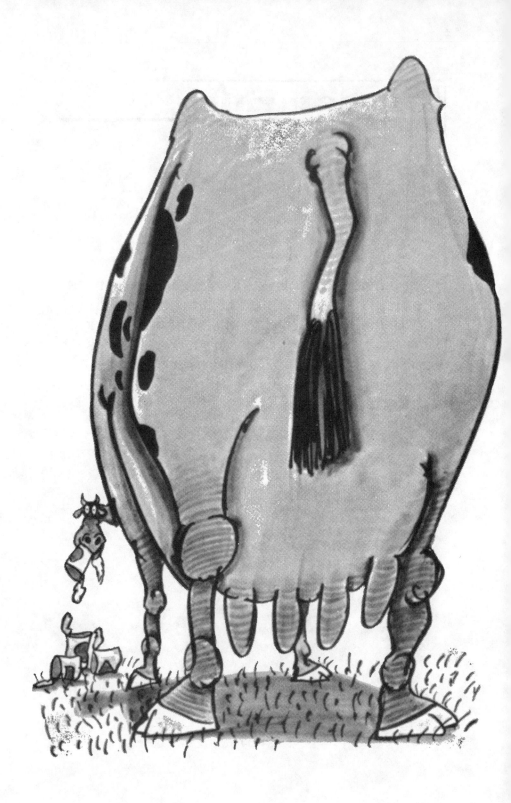

The Company Policy

If you walk in your office one day and find your family photos reframed, a potted palm where your teddy bear used to be, and all your pencils pointing magnetic north, don't bother asking. Anything that weird has got to be the work of the Company Policy. Company Policies are crosses between Scapegoats and Sacred Cows. They are born of individual shortcomings, sanctified by the weight of tradition, and every company keeps one to explain the inexplicable.

Like Nuns and Heroin Addicts, Company Policies are creatures of habit. These animals are living proof that you don't need brains in business provided your quirks, prejudices, and neuroses are moneymakers to begin with.

If you can't find anything on this page,
it is because Bonuses are very often invisible.

The Bonus

Bonuses are small, sickly animals that are often rumored to be larger and healthier than they really are. In most corporations, there is an ordinance against Bonuses running around loose, and so they are always tied to a Profit.

WARNING: Bonuses are the stuff dreams are made of; therefore, most of these creatures will vanish overnight.

The Pink Slip

There is nothing funny about this animal.

The Kick-Back

Kick-Backs are nocturnal animals that live in plain white envelopes. They make popular pets, but they are difficult to keep, because they tend to leave traces around the house that have to be covered up.

Many people find the name "Kick-Back" distasteful and prefer to call these animals something else. Construction companies call them Development Fees; MBAs call them Competitive Advantages; Japanese ministers call them Lockheeds.

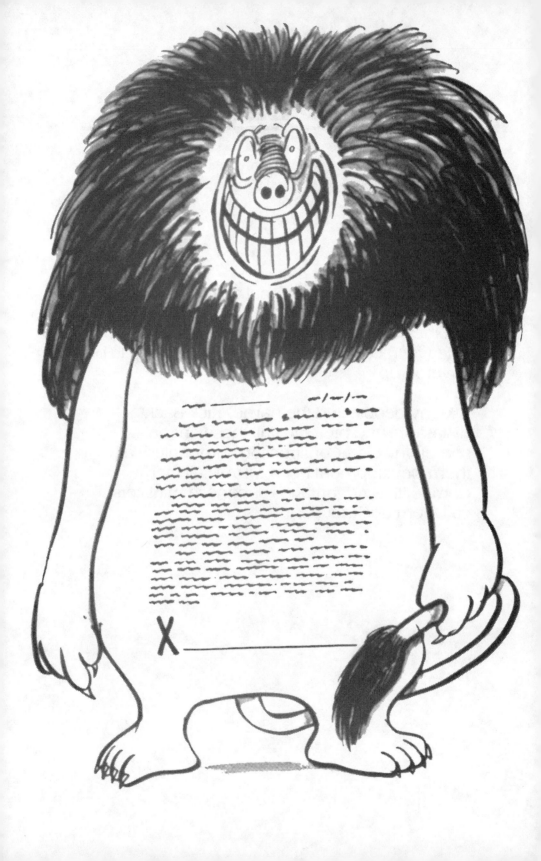

X _____

The Unsigned Contract

This is one of the most peculiar beasts in the business jungle. The Unsigned Contract has no apparent reason to exist, and its very existence implies the presence of absence, but it remains extremely common just the same.

If handled with great care, an Unsigned Contract can sometimes be domesticated into a Binding Contract. More often, however, it turns into that melancholy and duplicitous creature, the Handshake Agreement. This sad transformation has been known to ruin everything from giant multi-nationals right down to the rug.

Unsigned Contracts are unusual in that they are alternately hot-blooded and cold-blooded. Eventually they give birth, not to live young, but to dead young, by a process known as Breach of Contract.

Riders

Riders are slippery beasts that attach themselves to Contracts much as Barnacles cling to Whales. Riders are interesting because they have the surprising ability to reverse the direction of their host animal. Whenever you see a Contract that appears to be swimming in circles, you can be sure there are plenty of Riders attached.

The Mortgage

Mortgages are interesting animals. They are more common as house pets than Cats or Dogs, in spite of the fact that they can eat you out of the very house and home you needed them for in the first place. The standard variety of Mortgage is the Long-Term, but recently other breeds have been developed, such as the Variable-Rate Mortgage (also known as Bank Insurance), the Wrap-Around Mortgage (also known as the Stranglehold), and the Balloon Mortgage (known to creditors as the Bullet Mortgage or the Lead Balloon).

The Mortgage is unique in that it is the only animal that grows smaller as it matures, although waiting for this to happen can be like watching the grass grow.

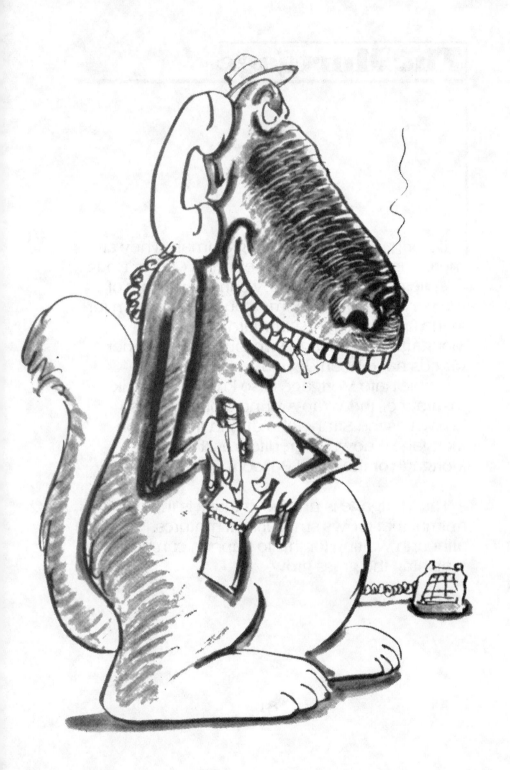

The D&B

The D&B is like the common cold: you get one periodically whether you want one or not. D&B's are typically dun colored, which Webster's describes as a dull, grayish brown. They hear better than Bats, and they have long snouts, which they like to keep in other people's business. Like Cats, they are insatiably curious, but unlike Cats, this seems to be no threat to their livelihood.

These beasts are extraordinarily polite unless they are provoked, and nothing provokes them more than not knowing everything about you. The D&B believes that knowledge exists to be shared. Businessmen prefer not to tell the D&B anything at all, because this is definitely an animal that kisses and tells.

The Clout

Clouts are like Suggestions, but have more money. They are very large animals with short tempers and long memories. No two Clouts are alike, but they are not hard to identify, because they always make a point of telling you just who they are.

Few people actually have one of these animals, but almost everyone claims to know somebody who does. The truth is that the individuals who do own these beasts like to keep quiet about it. In most cases, you don't know who really has the Clout until after the Clout has already had you.

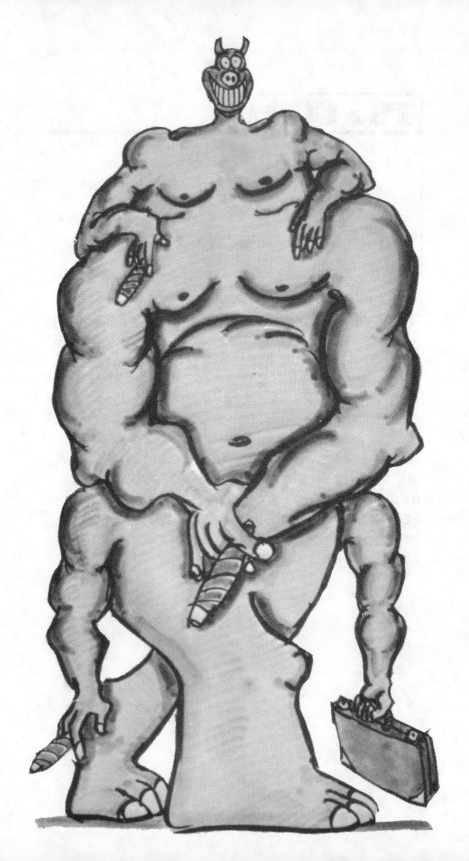

The Conglomerate

Conglomerates are beasts that have hard, wooden heads, known as boards, and many extremities of various sizes, which are called subsidiaries. Conglomerates, though powerful creatures, are sometimes slow-moving and frequently slow-witted. They have mountainous bodies over which they exercise partial control, and some of them are so big that they occupy space in several countries at the same time.

Recently some Conglomerates have been seen to actually decrease in size like the Incredible Shrinking Man by a surgical procedure known as Divestiture. These operations are often purely cosmetic.

The Monopoly

Monopolies are beasts that love to corner marketplaces. They are immensely influential in the financial world. Some of the most monopolistic include O P E C, A.T.&T., and the United States Mint.

Very few animals wear clothes. Monopolies, however, are sometimes seen in anti-trust suits. Monopolies wake up big in the morning and get bigger all day, and it goes without saying that they have unlimited growth potential.

The Competition

Like Skunks and Giant Squid, this is an animal nobody wants to be in back of. Staying ahead of this beast is not easy, however, because the Competition moves very quickly.

It is often difficult to tell just how big the Competition is, but it is usually described as "heavy." It is also occasionally called "friendly" and "healthy," but this is probably wishful thinking. Competitions are clever animals, and no sooner do you have an original idea than the Competition has it, too. In fact, sometimes the Competition is so good, it has your idea before you do.

The Preferred Customer

The Preferred Customer doesn't ask for estimates, understands inevitable delays, and pays in advance with a certified check. The Preferred Customer is an imaginary animal.